The Kraken's Revenge

Will Macmillan Jones

First edition 2022 by Red Kite Publishing Limited

Text Copyright 2022 by Will Macmillan Jones

Find out more about the author on
www.willmacmillanjones.com

ISBN: 9798449601407

CONTENTS

OTHER BOOKS BY WILL MACMILLAN JONES

The Space Scout Collection:

Scout Pilot of The Free Union

Infinity is for Losers

Rogue Pilot

Interstellar Mercenary

Galactic Fugitive

Star Spy

Paranormal Mysteries

The Mister Jones; Mysteries Collection

The Showing

Portrait of a Girl

The House Next Door

The Curse of Clyffe House

Demon's Reach

Fantastically Funny Fantasy:

The Banned Underground Collection

Tolkien meets Spinal Tap!

Red Kite Pocket Horror

For children:
Snort and Wobbles
Return of The Goblins

The Kraken's Revenge

The cove was named Smugglers'
Cove. A common enough name,
indeed this coast probably boasted
more coves and inlets of that name
that the real smugglers had ever
considered using. But the name
attracted the tourists and brought
in their spending money and for
those who lived on the coats, that
was more important than mere
historical accuracy. Besides, there
had been – perhaps still were –
real smugglers on the coast and so
the name was rather more honest
than the average political

broadcast and the locals lost no sleep over the matter. Nor did those who had bought holiday homes overly concern themselves with the local legends – except, perhaps, for a few who still took to the water on a fine day with a fishing line or net, or those who could trace their local family lineage back into the past.

Sailors are a superstitious bunch and the ghostly stories were embellished and enhanced beyond all recognition and rarely taken seriously: but seriously enough for that bay to be left alone. The reputation was of course sufficient attraction to draw teenagers to the warm sands in an evening and despite the misgivings of parents and older folk, the occasional party was held on the beach at Smugglers' Cove. Perhaps the loud music was not to the taste of whatever lived off the cove (if indeed anything did) argued the young: and spent time there with ghetto blasters and decks, drink and portable barbeques.

Perhaps those parties were observed by unseen eyes? Listened to by unseen ears? The scent of the fires and cooking carried to unseen nostrils?

The old tales of a forgotten monster were fun, to be retold in disbelief and the laughter of teenagers. Most especially they were fun at or close to All Hallows Eve: and what better time was there for a party on a haunted beach than Halloween? So the plans were laid and the invitations went out to The Kraken's Revenge Disco.

The locals were inclined to lose sleep -perhaps in advance – over the posters that appeared overnight one Saturday morning. Smugglers' Cove was a small hamlet of perhaps two or three dozen houses clustered around what had once been a genuine fisherman's tavern and a local shop.

The houses were small, built low against the prospect of sea gales. Many of the rooves were slate rather than tile and in the frequent storms, when rain lashed at the cottages huddled before the violence of nature, the houses resembled a clutch of seals lying on the shore. Some of the houses were still homes, but a small majority were now expensively acquired holiday homes or let properties catering for summer visitors.

There was but one road into the Cove. A few local routes existed too, but these possessed no signposts and se were avoided or dismissed by those who did not know the area. The probability of becoming hopelessly lost in a warren of lanes, all with high hedges precluding any chance of seeing any landmarks, was far too high.

The one road capable of bearing motorised traffic down to the harbour ran round the outside of the village, past the long beach and a car park. Before passing the beach, the road went past the solitary church. This building had been desanctified some years before and sold to a nameless property company. The small churchyard, with the many gravestones marking the last resting places – and in some cases only a memorial for souls lost at sea and not recovered – had been fenced off and lay undisturbed, poorly maintained, and overgrown. The locals had expected the building to be expensively converted to a holiday property, but for no known reason it had been left in its original condition.

Occasionally, a small group would arrive from out of town and lights would flicker and flame inside the building, to what end or purpose no one knew for none of the visitors stayed locally or were to be seen the following morning.

The posters perturbed the residents, and the visitors who were in the Cove so early in the season. Cheaply printed, crudely designed in gharish colours, they proclaimed a nightmare; a beach party and disco on the night of the spring equinox. The Kraken's Revenge disco. What a strange name, an ill-omened name for the remaining residents who recalled the traditions and legends of the sea. Still, perhaps few would be prepared to brave the spring weather, possibly the rain, and party on a beach.

The owner of the local shop

however had a more nuanced, or conflicted, view on matters and ordered a larger than normal delivery of alcoholic drinks. If the village had to suffer this intrusion, he reasoned, there was no reason not to make the best of it.

The night before the dreaded visitation, something unusual happened. The owners of the old church arrived, and remarkably had taken one of the holiday cottages for the weekend. They came in expensive imported cars, and one large van. They kept themselves to themselves, until darkness fell. Then lights, fitful at first then stronger, blazed within the old church building.

Music could be heard from within. Strange, discordant music that brought with it wild visions and unholy thoughts in those who heard it as they walked past the church. Those locals or visitors who heard the sounds hurried on past to their destination or homes, keen to leave the occupants to their own devices. No one tried to approach the church or stand on tiptoe to peer through the arched and mullioned windows to view the activity inside.

The combination of the insistent music that somehow stayed in the listener's head and the large van with the strange and disturbing image, evocative of an earlier age, were enough to discourage casual trespassing or enquiry.

The revelry, if such it was rather than a ceremony of a nature beyond the normal range of experience, continued until the early hours before, unwitnessed, the occupants closed and locked the property.

The following morning, the worst fear of the locals was confirmed for the dawn broke clear and bright over Smugglers' Cove. By midday, the shop was busy with teenagers buying drinks and snacks. The streets were full, and the staff behind the bar of the only pub weary from constantly refusing to sell alcohol to teenagers they considered clearly underage to drink. The only car park was full of cars, except for one corner near the sand where a large white van was parked somewhat inconsiderately. The day wore on, the late afternoon approached, and music began to play on the beach. Not yet the deranged yet exhilarating sounds played the night before. The music came from a hundred radios or phones, mixing tracks and styles.

Lights began to spring up along the beach as the sun fell towards the sea. The light from the sun reflected on the waters, forming a highway from the horizon to the beach. It was, in the considered view of the passengers on the small yacht cruising slowly towards the small cove, unutterably beautiful. The dancers on the beach admired the yacht as they would a painting on a spare wall and forgot it.

The waters off the cove were deserted. Despite the name, and the implied promise of a safe harbour for small ships, the approach to this particular Smugglers' Cove was dangerous: a tidal race with strange currents, hidden sandbanks, and often barely concealed rocks posed risks for amateur yachtsmen that most declined, seeking more welcoming shores.

Accordingly, the small bay was shunned or ignored by the local sailing fraternity. And of course, there were the rumours – normally spoken quietly late at night in the bar, of something unnamed that disliked sailors and those who were unwise enough to venture into the bay and anchor there might not be seen again.

Whatever lived below the waters of the cove would take revenge for the intrusion. A rumour of course that was laughed at in the broad daylight, a nighttime story to scare children or pass a pleasant hour before the fire.

*

The yacht nosed slowly into the bay, the sail taking the onshore breeze and using it to move closer to the shore. One of the crew lay on the bow, peering down into the water for sunken rocks and calling directions. The beach was beginning to fill with happy, laughing teenagers and as the sun dropped to the horizon, the bonfire on the beach was lit. Sparks rose and flew in the small breeze. As the yacht dropped anchor, the music rose in volume.

"Come on, last one to the beach is a loser!" shouted Mark, the owner of the yacht. He tied down the sail and leapt over the side into the sea. Steph, his girlfriend, whooped with delight and followed him. The other two waited long enough to drag off jeans and tshirts and then joined them.

"Mark! What about the beers!" shouted Paul as he splashed in the water towards the beach. While Steph was swimming to the sand the waters were shallow enough for Paul to wade towards the beach with a bag held up over his head.

Predictably Mark reached the beach first and climbed out onto the sand where he posed to show off his physique. Steph arrived moments later, panting and scrabbling on all fours through the surf until she stood upright and laughing.

"Where's the beer?" demanded Mark.

"Coming!" called Paul.

Across the sand a group of older boys were setting up a music system and decks on a table and pulling enthusiastically on the cord to start the generator that would run the amplifiers and speakers. Success at last crowned their efforts, and the beach began to vibrate softly but steadily to the pulse of the bass. Through the sand to the rocks below, out into the water of the cove and further out to the wider seas ran the beat, disturbing the creatures that lived below the waves; perhaps waking others from dreamless sleep. The beat ran as a counter pulse to the steady rhythm of the sea, creating small eddies that ran and flowed within the cove. As the sun fell below the horizon so the moon rose, spreading a cold silvery light across the beach.

More and more teenagers ran onto the sands and danced and sang below the moon. Out across the bay light glimmered and flashed on the breaking waves and if they did so in a pattern that might have suggested something other than hidden rocks below the surface, something that moved slowly and observed rather than was itself observed.

Paul pulled on some warmer clothing, and passed some to his girlfriend, Lucy. She too had swum from Mark's boat to the beach and so was grateful for a sweatshirt and jeans. She drank another can as the music swirled.

"Steady on!" Paul said. "You aren't used to alcohol."

"The way you are?" she asked.

Paul reacted to the implied criticism. "Well, that's because…"

"Because what?" Lucy looked around. The beach was full of teenagers dancing and laughing and drinking. The crowd around the DJ and his decks was mostly male. Perhaps she would find a better option than Paul, who was beginning to annoy her with his patronising attitude. "Because I'm a girl?"

"I didn't mean it that way."

Lucy turned and flounced off across the beach towards the DJ. Paul started after her, but Mark caught his arm.

"Let her go."

"But Mark!"

"Just let her go. There's always another girl around."

"Mark, you know how I feel about her." Paul gazed after Lucy, who was striding faster across the beach now that she was annoyed that Paul wasn't following her. The DJ turned on a house style dance song and Lucy began to skip across the sands.

"Yeah, and you're daft. Look around you. There's loads of girls. Just go and get one."

Paul was annoyed by Mark's attitude and stared after Lucy until he lost sight of her in the party. "I'm going back to the boat."

"Yacht. She's a *yacht*, Paul, and don't you forget it."

Paul thought his friend's voice sounded a little sour. Perhaps he had already had more to drink than he should. Instead of replying, he nodded and walked off towards the surf. He was taken aback when a kick on his ankles suddenly swept his feet out from under him and a hand hit him in the middle of his back. Startled he fell, falling into the water with a splash.

"Don't touch anything, and stay out of my bunk," ordered Mark, looking down at Paul as he struggled in the surf.

Steph had been waiting nearby, but she just giggled at Paul's discomfiture and turned away, back to the arty on the beach. Paul wouldn't look at her, just waded out into the shallows, keeping a careful eye on the boat. It wouldn't do to miss the mark. Not that he'd miss Mark after this. This was one insult too far. The tide was further in now and he had to raise his head to breathe. Paul carried on, until with relief he grabbed at the side of the yacht. But was it the yacht? Whatever he had grabbed did not feel like wood. It was hard and smooth, but somehow felt more organic.

This felt like living, rather than dead wood. Then it began to move under his hand. Paul opened his mouth to scream for help but cold salt water filled it choking off his voice. Darkness, blacker still against the night sky, filled his vision. He struck out vainly, hitting only the cold sea: something took hold of his arm and his nostrils filled with a cold, unclean scent reminiscent of dead seaweed and rotting things As he was pulled below the waves he heard the pounding drum n bass from The Kraken's Revenge disco swell in his ears.

*

On the beach Lucy was dancing in the crowd of boys surrounding the decks. The DJ had turned up the volume, careless of any complaints from the local residents in the nearby village sheltered behind the dunes. Before the police could get themselves sorted out to deal with the 'noise nuisance', The Kraken's Revenge disco would be over and he would be gone.

"My name's Lucy!" Lucy had to shout into the ear of a cute boy she had met in the crowd.

"I'm James!" He still had a jacket on and he reached inside a pocket and took out a small flat bottle. "Drink?"

Lucy nodded. She took the bottle from James, unscrewed the cap and drank. She handed back the bottle. James drank from it then put the cap back on and out the bottle back in his pocket.

"Keep some for later, when it goes cold," he told her.

She smiled and waved at him then darted through the crowd to the DJ. He was standing at the record and CD decks set up on a trestle table. A small group surrounded him, shouting and drinking while the DJ largely ignored them, concentrating on the music flooding out through the large speakers of his PA system. Lucy thought about speaking to him but seeing the look of ferocious concentration upon his face changed her mind. Steph was there, dancing on her own. She was barefoot on the sands, a light skirt swirling about her legs. Her eyes were closed, and Mark was nowhere to be seen. Lucy came up to her and Steph's eyes opened and flashed with recognition.

"Dance!" shouted Steph, "Dance!"

"Where's Mark?"

"Who cares? This is amazing! Bring on The Kraken!"

The music changed to a heavier, darker beat. Now it was pierced, punctuated, by a chant: "The Kraken's Revenge! The Kraken's Revenge!" If anyone had been present at the church the night before to listen, they would have recognised this music.

Steph joined in the chanting. Looking round, Lucy could see that most of the crowd had their hands in the air and were repeating the words in a meaningless cycle. Just behind her, shouting with the others was the boy who had called himself James. Quite attractive, at least in the dark, she thought.

Wordlessly he pushed the bottle of spirits at her and she took it with a pantomime kiss. James tried to put an arm around her waist to pull her close. Laughing, she wagged a finger in his face in coquettish rejection. James laughed back. In return she took his hand and started to run across the dark beach.

Changing, the music faltered briefly. In that moment Lucy thought she heard a cry from out across the dark sea. She drank from the bottle of spirits James had given her and felt her senses swim and her remaining inhibitions dissolve. She still held James' hand and pulled him further towards the darkest and unoccupied end of the beach. Here the sands themselves seemed to vibrate to the beat.

There was a deep fissure, a trench perhaps, scored into the beach as if to mark the passage of some leviathan, or maybe the track caused by pulling a fishing vessel up onto the beach for safety. The sand was damp, a result of the occasional wave rolling up the channel.

Lucy stumbled and fell. James fell on top of her, pulled down by her clutching hand, and laughing together they rolled into the edge of the surf. James kissed Lucy again and this time she did not resist. His hands slipped beneath her clothing; questing, seeking, and this too she did not resist: but gasped in pleasure.

James froze.

"Don't stop! Don't stop now!" cried Lucy.

"Did you hear something?"

Lucy listened, then grabbed at his hands. "No! There's nothing here but us, the music and the darkness."

"There it is again." James rolled away from Lucy and sat up.

"Look, if you don't want to, I'm sure I can find someone who does!"

"Shut up. There's someone here. Nearby."

Lucy lay still. Now a creeping fear replaced her earlier sensuality.

"What? Who is it?"

The sea heaved, the surf hissed and they caught the sound of a single, harsh breath. An unearthly sound to chill the bones.

"What's that?" Lucy clung to James.

James twisted around trying to see who was breathing like that. What was breathing like that. Like something only from the pit of his nightmares, drawn here to this beach under the cold moonlight to instill terror and dread, and succeeding. He strained against the darkness but could see nothing. Even the stars had vanished.

The breath, a deep rattling sound, as if the breather was unused to the air itself, to the environment of the beach, perhaps even to life – and despised all three to the depths of its being, was close by.

"Run!" James was on his feet, pulling at Lucy's hand.

"Which way?" she asked. "Which way?" There was only one way. Back towards the flames of the bonfire, back to the pounding music, back to the drinking and laughing on the beach, back to the party and the safety and security of friends. Away from the darkness and the unknown.

James' hand slid from her grasp. Salt spray from the waves brushed her fingertips, making her jump. First a muffled grunt: then the sound of some enormous bulk dragging itself across the sands. The harsh breathing came again but now heavy with satisfaction and somehow replete. The seas parted with a sigh, barely a splash.

"James?" she asked uncertainly. When there was no reply, she called his name again: once, twice, then shouting, demanding. There was no reply other than the soft voice of the surf. Lucy stood, took a step towards the distant lights and fell again. Three deep marks scored across the sands immediately in front of her, the sign of the passage of – something. Her bare foot hit something. She bent down to pick it up and realised that it was a shoe. With a cry of horror, she realised the shoe still held his foot and ankle.

Lucy dropped the shoe and threw up, vomiting everything she had drunk. For a mad moment she thought she should take the shoe back to the party, but she could not face picking it up again, if indeed she could find it again in the darkness. She wiped her mouth, put a hand into the sea and splashed the welcome, clean, salty water across her face; then stumbled away, back to the party.

"The Kraken's Revenge! The Kraken's Revenge!" rang out again across the sands from the PA and Lucy giggled in incipient hysteria before pushing her way deep into the dancing crowd.

*

Mark had found some like-minded friends and as a result had become very drunk. He searched the dancing beach party for Steph, his eyes bleary and unfocussed. He could not walk in a straight line and kept bumping into others on the beach. To some he apologised, at others he shouted abuse.

Unable to find his girlfriend, he decided to seek out Paul. That was what friends were for after all, to commiserate with each other over girls. Where was Paul? Mark dimly recalled a spat with his friend and Paul storming off.

He hadn't seen him since, now that he came to think about it. Where would Paul go? It had to be the yacht. That was it. He'd go to his yacht, get on board and sleep off the drink with Paul. Then, in the morning, they would raise sail, leave the cove and sail home. The music from the speakers hammered across the sands and out across the cove, and Mark followed in its wake.

The sea water was cold as it rose towards his knees, and he staggered at the sudden force of the sea as it pushed against him. Stopping him. The sea was stopping him from reaching his yacht. Well, he was stronger than the sea, better than the sea and everything in it.

He would wade out to the yacht against the scend of the sea! He was the stronger. That piece of floating driftwood, that was nothing, nothing, compared to him. A log perhaps. But between him and his yacht, so he strode on towards where he thought it was moored. There, the driftwood was sliding away from him, behind him. An omen, a sign. The sea was strong but he, Mark, was stronger. The driftwood surged, banged against his thigh. Annoying. Mark reached down to shove the log away. The log wouldn't move and he grew angry with it. He hit the log, hurting his hand and he swore.

He pushed at the log again and

it moved. But not away from him. This time the log scraped its way up his side, cutting him badly. Blood oozed from the cuts and abrasions. The log continued to grow. As it rose above his head Mark looked up in wonderment into a pair of eyes that glowed red as angry coals, red as rubies, red as fire, red as revenge. Below the eyes were teeth, teeth that were as red as the pain in his side, red as the blood that dripped from his chest, red as the torn flesh he saw when he looked down at his chest.

Mark toppled backwards into the cold water, his ears filled with the chanting from the beach: 'The

Kraken's Revenge! The Kraken's Revenge!'

*

On the beach the music rose again, to the general dismay of the local residents. Several tried ringing the police emergency line and were brusquely told to get off the phone and make way for a real emergency. Those who tried the non-emergency line were met with sympathy, but no practical help. Disgusted, although not surprised, they hung up and tried their best to shut out the noise, while hoping that any teenage children they may have were not present on the beach.

Inside the de consecrated church, a green light rose from the old stone altar, casting eldritch shadows among the rafters. The stained-glass windows took on a change aspect from the unearthly, unholy, light. The faces of the saints immortalised in the glass now held a greenish cast that changed their appearance. Those that had been kindly, they became callous. Those figures represented as stern of visage became malevolent or harsh. The light grew deeper in hue, phantasmagorical, somehow monstrous. The green light filled the building, turning the water in the ancient font a bilious, unhealthy, even impious hue.

No worshipper was present. No one walked the central isle inside the nave, no one strolled outside the building, so no one could witness the vile excrescence that slowly started to form on the altar. A deeper green than the light generated around it at present it had no form, no shape, no confirmed physical presence here in this reality. Yet if anyone had been present inside to witness this ancient rite moving inexorably towards its climax, they would have needed no explanation, no well-reasoned argument, to believe that it was alive in some way and absolutely was self-aware: and did not in any sense belong here.

*

Amy lived in the village. Her parents were some of those who had tried in vain to seek help from the authorities. She didn't care. The music was great, her friends were around her and everyone was having fun. There was very little alcohol needed, she knew how to get high on the music alone.

Some of her friends were drunk, one was very drunk. He had fallen to his knees in the swaying crowd. She laughed at him, and he grinned back at her. Amy looked up as a girl pushed roughly past her. The girl was swaying rather than dancing, her face distraught and fearful.

"Had too much," Amy said to herself. Should she ask this stranger if she needed help? That would be normal for Amy, to offer support to a fellow human. But at that moment the music changed, the girl moved on into the whirling throng and the moment slid away as the crowd moved. Amy found herself alone and decided to push through the dancers towards the DJ. A random youth offered her a packet of white powder: smiling she declined.

"Go on, it will get you into the beat, into the groove."

"No thanks, I'm already there."

"Come on, you can't have fun without some of this, sister."

Amy stepped back. A kissing couple locked in a deep clinch reeled between her and the dealer and she was away. Through the crowd she could make out the tables holding the decks. It just meant moving in the direction of the speakers whose volume at this distance was almost painful. The two youths dancing right in front of one of the speaker stacks would have hearing difficulties afterwards, she was sure.

A rope strung between the speakers marked a line that the revelers were not supposed to pass to reach the DJ and the crew. The table holding the decks and mixers had a huge banner strung below it. In lurid green paint, some strange creature from the depths was depicted with the legend 'The Kraken's Revenge' in what she thought was a gothic script.

Amy drew attention wherever she went. She certainly drew the attention of some of the DJ, who beckoned her over to the decks, then drew her behind the line of the speakers so that they could speak.

"This is great!" enthused Amy.

"You like it? That's great!"

"Even better than last month!"

"You think so?"

"Yes! Look at how many people have come down."

"We were worried that people might not come."

"Why?" asked Amy.

"Well, we heard that a couple of guys went missing." The DJ eyed Amy carefully.

"Probably eloped or something." Amy was not bothered.

"You reckon?"

"Who cares? Nothing ever happens here, this rave is great!"

"Want to come back after?"

"Where?"

"That old church. We bought it as a base for the stuff, so that we can gig here and all around this area easily. It's kind of cool, don't you think? Like a church for music, something older, more real."

"Oh, I can't tonight. The oldies would moan at me too much. But next month if you're back?"

"Oh, we'll be back. Make sure you come and see us. Look, here's a pass." The DJ handed Amy a small square card embossed with the same image as the sign below the decks.

"Thanks! See you then!" Amy whirled away.

The DJ watched her thoughtfully. Not tonight, then. Patience. Next month, in the de consecrated church, he could summon the other Old One. That one had waited centuries, another four weeks wouldn't make a difference. He knew that the light in the church would now be fading, the writing figure on the profaned altar returning to the void from which it had come.

*

Empty, desolate and abandoned, the yacht rocked, pulling against the anchor. An arm, thick as a tree trunk, smashed down across the cabin, pushing through to the very keel. The mast toppled and the hungry sea poured into the hull. The waters heaved, the yacht and the dark shape were gone; the beach party over. The DJ and his crew packed away the PA system as the teenagers left the beach. Then, from a drawer in the boxes of CDs he removed two items.

One was a scarf embroidered with strange and arcane symbols; this he draped around his neck. The second was a full bottle of spirits. Uncorking this he walked slowly to the edge of the water and after raising both arms in the air, the DJ poured a silent libation to the Old God, the forgotten God: The Kraken. The Kraken whose revenge was complete – for now

The Painted Doorknob

Completion of the house sale, or rather purchase, had been delayed – but had finally gone through. Robert collected the keys from the man in charge of the removal men at the front door of the house, and was mildly surprised at his abrupt refusal to enter the property.

The refusal did not extend to those under his authority however, and the foreman waved at the other men quite brusquely to get on with the task of unloading Robert's possessions from the very large van parked at the end of the drive. The driver had not wished to reverse closer to the front door, something that had made Robert wonder about the firm that he had employed. They had been a little reluctant to take the commission, but Robert had been prepared to pay the fee requested.

"Are you sure you don't fancy a cup of tea?" he asked as the removal men pushed past them and dropped the heavy boxes that represented Robert's worldly possessions in the rooms that approximated their final destinations. Robert wondered if they were in a hurry, or if they normally worked at this pace.

Perhaps removals was a highly pressured business? In any event, some of the boxes and smaller items of furniture were being quite roughly handled and Robert made a mental note to examine everything and make a damages list for a possible subsequent claim.

"No thanks," replied the foreman. "You're quite brave, buying this place – especially at this time of year."

"What do you mean?"

"Well, it's this time of year that something spooky happens here. Mostly it's just noise, but last Halloween the owner disappeared. I suppose the estate agent didn't tell you anything about that, did they?"

"Not a thing."

"Should have done, really. Isn't there a law about that now? Anyway, the last one who lived here, he vanished one Halloween night they say. No trace of him ever found, there wasn't. His family turned up, looked at the place, and none of them wanted to live in it. Sensible of them. Didn't you Google the place before you bought it? Or even ask any of the neighbours? We were all a bit surprised when it sold so easily. The we guessed you were not from round here, as no one local would want to live in this house."

Robert looked around the hall. It was quite bright, and the house felt entirely peaceful, with not the slightest hint of any threat. "I didn't see any reason not to," he replied. "Saw the place online, liked it and got it at a decent price."

"Well good luck to you!" said the foreman. "Living here alone, is it? No family?"

"On my own," Robert agreed. "Divorced and looking forward to some peace and quiet after that."

"Well good luck with that," said the foreman again. His men finished unloading with what Robert now saw as indecent haste, and they all left without waiting for the customary tip. Robert was left alone in his new home: a home that felt quiet and welcoming but which now, in his head, held a dark undercurrent. A sudden sense of unease filled him, then slipped away.

The week before Halloween passed without incident, and Robert decided that the removal men had been winding him up. The house had the usual issues experienced by any new homeowner unused to the idiosyncrasies of a property, and Robert found that he enjoyed discovering these and dealing with them.

It took him three days of searching before he came to the

conclusion that the house possessed no internal stop cock to shut off the water supply. He found that he had to lie flat on the damp pavement outside the front gate and reach down under an access flap to close the main supply valve in order to shut off the water and repair a dripping tap.

There were occasional noises at night under the stairs and in the attic: but every time Robert went (sometimes, to his private shame, with a cricket bat!) to investigate, he found nothing. The most annoying thing about the house was the central heating, which needed coaxing into life on a regular basis. As the evenings grew colder with the ending of the year, he needed the central heating on and each night he had to descend the unsteady wooden steps to the cellar floor to relight the boiler and get hot water flowing around the house into the radiators. Once the system was working, the house quickly became warm and comfortable but until then the rooms all carried an unpleasant chill.

Halloween came, cold and wet and stormy. By six in the evening, the house was becoming too cold for comfort. The boiler needed relighting before the cellar became too dark to see to press the reset switch, and so Robert made his careful way down into the cellar and relit the boiler: then he clambered back up the stairs and stopped to take a deep breath. Each time he had gone down the stairs he had done so with some trepidation followed by a strong feeling of relief when he emerged back on the ground floor without accident.

The stairs would need repair work very soon, and he hoped that he would not have to venture back into the cellar until he had got tradesmen in to make the stairs properly safe.

Opposite the door to the cellar was another door. Clearly it was a storage door as it was set underneath the stairs to the upper story. Robert had tried to open the door once, but the collection of keys that he had been given didn't seem to have one that fitted that door.

Tilting his head to one side in puzzlement, he looked at the door: something today was different, he decided. He stared at the cupboard door and then realised that the peeling black paint on the door knob was suddenly a bright yellow. He looked at the knob, perplexed. It had definitely been black yesterday, he thought. Reaching out he gingerly touched the bright yellow knob.

Robert wasn't sure what to expect, but the wooden door knob felt just as it should. He took firm hold and twisted the knob. It turned, but the door didn't open. He pushed and pulled: the door shifted and rattled, but remained obstinately shut.

Determined to solve the puzzle, Robert left the cupboard and went to the front door of the house. Beside the door was a small hall table with a bowl on it. In the bowl lay the collection of keys that had come from the agents acting for the family of the last owner. He picked up the keys and went back to the cupboard. One by one he tried each of the keys in the lock. None fitted.

He stared at the yellow door knob, shrugged of the mystery and turned away. As he did so he heard a rattling noise behind the cupboard door. Faint at first it grew steadily louder. Robert raised his hand and touched the door nervously – the sound stopped at once.

"Hello?" Robert felt silly calling out. He knew there was no one else in this house. "Hello?" There was, of course, no reply and for a moment Robert wondered what he would have done if someone had answered. After turning away he glanced back – the doorknob was once again a somber, peeling, black.

A mystery, he decided and actually felt rather pleased with the idea that the house really was not as bland and uninteresting as the flat he had himself just sold. The removal man's hints and vague warnings he discounted as the superstitions of an uneducated man – or alternatively a clumsy attempt to tease a newcomer to the area.

The next evening the boiler once again refused to start. The daylight was fading now in the early evening as autumn took a hold on the world, and the golden evening light gave only an illusion of warmth. The house felt uncomfortably cool, so Robert again drew a deep breath and descended the steps into the cellar, vowing to call an engineer the next day.

The boiler relit with a loud 'whoomph', causing him to step backwards: but then it settled down, the blue control light casting an eerie glow across the stone floor. He took hold of the stairs' banister and felt the wood move unsteadily under his hand. He put one foot on the lowest step, but that seemed secure. Cautiously he tried the next step, then the one after. Slowly and carefully he climbed the stairs towards the door, not trusting the banister rail which now seemed to tremble with every step.

As he reached the top of the flight of stairs the whole structure felt unstable and with a gasp he grabbed at the half closed cellar door. It would not do to fall, to be hurt, on his own in his house and so far from a telephone. The single window in the cellar was set too high in the wall to be reached if the stairs did collapse leaving him with a sprained ankle, or maybe worse. For a moment, an image of himself trapped, hurt, in the cellar as the night closed in flashed before his eyes and he shivered.

The cellar door was reassuringly solid. He grasped it with some relief, and tried to still the pounding of his racing heart. Pulling the door open made the top step again sway under his feet and with some relief Robert staggered out of the darkening cellar into the last golden glow of the evening sun on the ground floor of the house, and fell onto his knees in the hall.

Looking up, his eyes were drawn to the cupboard door in front of him. The doorknob had again changed colour, this time to an unhealthy, livid, green: a somehow unpleasing shade. One he would repaint himself if it stayed, he thought.

Then he thought about that. That a door could change colour in this way was outside of his experience. How was it even possible? The warning hints from the removal men returned to alarm him, and he resolutely put them out of his mind.

This was a mystery, to be sure: but one that he could solve. One that he would solve. And without any mystical nonsense! The colour on the door was so unpleasant that he was reluctant to touch the doorknob at all.

But when something rattled behind the door he forced himself to grab hold of the knob and try to turn it. To his amazement, with a groan from the hinges, it opened slightly.

Surprised, Robert pulled the door open as far as possible. Inside the cupboard below the stairs, it was very dark. He could see nothing within. With a sudden compulsion he stepped inside the cupboard, into the space below the stairs.

His feet crunched on something in

the darkness, a darkness that seemed to fall heavily around him. Looking down he could see little, then as his eyes adjusted he saw that he was standing on a pile of bones.

He let out a cry and staggered backwards towards the door – but his back touched only an unexpected solid wall where the door should have been.

Then, glowing in the darkness, first one pair then another, then many more pairs of red-lit eyes came into view as the rats poured into the space below the stairs. Robert opened his mouth to scream.

Outside the cupboard the doorknob turned a somber, peeling black again. Robert's screams barely filtered through the door and entirely failed to disturb the quiet house while the rats fed and outside, the young children ran in the street dressed as ghouls, witches, ghosts, and zombies, demanding 'Trick or Treat!" from indulgent householders. None cared to knock at the door of the house as Robert suffered and died, and the prepared pile of sweets gleamed briefly in the last light of the day then faded into darkness.

ABOUT THE AUTHOR

Will Macmillan Jones lives in Wales, a lovely green, verdant land with a rich cultural heritage. He does his best to support this heritage by drinking the local beer and shouting loud encouragement whenever International Rugby is on the TV. A sixty something lover of blues, rock and jazz he has just fulfilled a lifetime ambition by filling an entire wall of his home office with (full) bookcases. When not writing or playing guitar with a group of friends, he is usually lost with the help of a SatNav on top of a large hill in the middle of nowhere, looking for dragons. He hasn't found one yet, but insists that it is only a matter of time.

He is known locally as a poet and oral storyteller, specializing in ghost stories and traditional tales, some of which can be found on YouTube, and others are now available to buy on CD.

www.ingramcontent.com/pod-product-compliance
Lightning Source LLC
Chambersburg PA
CBHW072048150726
47996CB00015B/2189